100 Punks Drool

by Cody Goodfellow

IN HINDSIGHT, THE EVOLUTION OF ANYTHING LOOKS LIKE A STEADY ASCENT, THE NEATLY STRATIFIED FOSSIL RECORD STACKED LIKE THE STEPS OF A GEOMETRY PROOF. EVEN THE END OF THE DINOSAURS IS JUST A METEORIC PERIOD AT THE END OF AN EON-LONG SENTENCE, BUT IT'S QUITE A DIFFERENT THING TO LIVE THROUGH IT, AND HARDER TO PICK WHICH CRAFTY MUTANTS WILL INHERIT THE EARTH.

As punk and disco demolished hippie rock and glam metal, so the SF New Wave heralded by Harlan Ellison's Dangerous Visions and the cinematic visions of 2001 and Star Wars revamped the heart and face of popular science fiction, which had been spinning in circles since the days of Flash Gordon. A decade later, Portland punk and renegade pulp writer John Shirley famously coined the term cyberpunk for the nascent literary movement that in turn rendered all that came before it quaint and ripe for extinction, and left us a handy suffix to slap onto any new twist in the formula.

But what does it mean to "punk" a genre?

Looking to the last major waves of disruption, cyberpunk reclaimed the future for the forgotten street people in much the same way hardboiled crime took murder back from the Agatha Christie set that treated murder like a parlor game. More than its visual style, it bestowed an ethos and an attitude—a new way to walk and talk, as Greil Marcus had it—that skewered the empty

Genre of Things that SF had become, while also indicting its rancid politics. SF's ray gun & opera-cape objectivist fever dreams of one selfish individual overturning sweaty dystopias were ripe fertilizer for the grimy reengagement with popular culture and class issues that Gibson, Sterling and Shirley (who appears in this issue!), et al, brought to the page.

Likewise, horror was still rehashing Gothic mediocrity until Levin, King, Rice and Koontz brought it up to date in the 70's; but they were already the staid establishment a decade later, when the "splat pack" showed up to wreck the place like a rock star's Holiday Inn suite.

But as with music, post-millennial genre fiction has nucleated, with countless niches riding their own cycles of stagnation and rebirth and very little monolithic change. If so inclined, you can marinate unironically in racist power fantasies like Howard, Burroughs and Talbot Mundy used to write, or party like Reagan never left with ultra-splatty extreme horror bereft of subtext or self-awareness. Cyberpunk zombies on long after its originators shot it in the face, as devoid of revolutionary grit as any other facet of the eternal vaporwave regurgitation of 80's aesthetics. But if you like your pulp crunchy and full of real surprises, the changes are brewing fast and furious in the primordial gutter of modern pulp.

Few movements have rekindled the punk spirit more ferociously than Bizarro, which started as a full-frontal DIY assault on all genre conventions that cleverly combined parody, absurdism and an earnest love of the pop culture trash they were burning. True to the core principles of earlier punk movements, bizarro zeroed in on our fantasy lives' ironic distance from, and troublesome enabling relationship with, shitty reality,

but even a punk af movement built on aggressively inverting reader expectations must inevitably collapse into itself and become Muzak the moment it succumbs to inertia and imitation.

By far, the most meaningful change currently underway in the latterday world of pulp is the explosion of diversity. From the New Weird to the Afrofuturist movements, BIPOC writers are turning the field inside out, reclaiming agency and power for previously muted or objectified groups in a way that reflexively casts grimdark fantasy, cyberpunk nihilism and Lovecraftian despair as obsolete luxury items for apathetic white males. Their contributions revitalize tired genre tropes and remind us why we fell in love with this stuff in the first place, but the old -punk label does them an injustice. (Forbidden Futures is fiercely committed to bringing more diversity to its own corner of the pulp underground with every issue, but we've come to acknowledge that we're like polka; our particular literary fetish is not as universally embraced as we might wish… but we're working on it.)

For this issue, we assembled a crack team of punks past and present—from John Shirley, who sprang out of the 60's New Wave to reintroduce adult human psychology to epic SF, to emergent renegades like Erica L. Satifka, John Wayne Comunale, and Nick Mamatas—to subvert and—punk (or at least funk) some familiar formulas. For far too long, pulp has been an escapist backwater; but in its dime-novel infancy, pulp thrived in times of real uncertainty, when people sought escape. But in times when escape is not an option, pulp must go on the offensive. The moment the frontier becomes a sandbox, or the jungle becomes a parking strip, it's time to move.

Follow us…

NAKED EXPRESSION
John Shirley

Killing is fulfilling if it's face to face; cyberspace milling doesn't end the race:
You have to smell the blood; have to taste...the blood.
—from Naked Expression, lyric by Jerome X, circa 2057

1

The avatorn happened on threedy chan 54255.b3, which was a veer that Kriss Liss thought no one but the Z-tranz cognoscenti knew.

But Lucius Schooner had slid around Annabel Lee, a Z-tranz girl; got her to whisk him there. Hence when Kriss was launching his threedy graffiti, Lucius bashed through it with a veer yacht, his VR craft The *Insistent Gargoyle* smashing Kriss's hard work asunder. On a whim Lucius had wrecked more than two months of Kriss's work—his *life*—as he told Annabel Lee, in a privacy pod an hour later.

"Oh don't be such a prima donna," she said. "You still have the model on file, you can run it any time."

"He smashed *the moment!* And it was..." He was glad his avatar wasn't set for emotion relay. He didn't want her to know he was almost sobbing. "That graff was a message to you! I was asking you to *deep* with me...veer and meat both."

Her avatar blinked; its sheath flickered uneasily. Her TruMe was mini-mono/goth fusion, black and magenta hair writhing sensuously, whiteless black eyes glistening, taut black lace dress displaying a pierced bleeding breast. Annabel loved extremes; he adored that about her. He wondered what she looked like in person. Rumor was: hot. "You shoulda gotten more serious with me earlier," she said. "I thought about you that way—but then Lucius said you were *meat-ugh* and you have a colostomy bag—"

"Lies!"

"And he took me to the High Charge, it's hard to get in but his Dad owns it—"

The High Charge. The most expensive VR body-feedback site in the world. How was he supposed to compete with that? *Fuck-ruck you Lucius.* Trillionaire dad fuck-fucker. And Kriss didn't know who his own dad was.

"Can I show you my threedy *now?*" Kriss asked. "It takes less than an hour to watch the whole thing. It's the best expression I ever did, Annabel. Seamless!"

Her avatar shook its head and put on a haughty-but-provocative look. "I promised to get back to the yacht, we're going to High Charge! Lucius's Dad's gonna let us sail right up into the middle of the club! I'm so *utterly* going to be there! If you want to *see-meat,* and all that, then you got to show me you're full hard-corpse!" Then—she vanished.

Kriss nodded. He'd see Annabel Lee got what she wanted.

2

Coming out of hook, Lucius Schooner felt the sickness from going more than three hours over health-bar. He muttered, "Fuck, Annabel, you are the queen of manipush…" He retched, and his head throbbed. He went to the bathroom, pissed up a storm, then showered the immersion reek off. He sighed, knowing he would be in trouble with Dad. He'd have to pay the fine. Since the two-hundred-thousand had starved to death, the laws about VR immersion were strict. And Dad lectured him about "a balance in life" and "you don't wanta turn into a jellyfish, boy…"

But Lucius's body was firm and strong, even if he felt kinda sick right now. He used the best designer 'roids and he did the VR workout that actually made his body meat-pump, so what's the big deal. He came out of the bathroom, naked, going to his dresser. . . .

"What the fuck is that?" Lucius stared at his fabber. The 3D printer—top of the line—was auto-printing. It shouldn't be on. And it was printing something that it should not be printing: little naked *dolls* of some kind, each about six inches long. Bunch of them, one after another, flopping out of the chute. They just lay there, piling up on the table. He walked over, thinking about running troubleshoot on the fabber, and suddenly the pile of little naked people wriggled…and one crawled out from under the others.

They're alive, he thought. Some hacker was using the banned biohack print-modeling. Micro neurology, behavioral programming; all kinds of sick shit.

There were now eighteen miniature, nude Kriss Lisses staring up at him; six-inch tall versions of the hacker; identical faces, identical expressions. Then—they opened their tiny mouths and gave out piping little shrieks and leapt as one, up onto his bare hip, crawling rapidly up him, fast as an amphetamined gecko, and he screamed and started slapping them off. But one of them grabbed the index finger of his right hand and bit down hard enough with its minuscule teeth so that pain and blood spurted and Lucius yelled and whipped his arm to throw the thing against the wall but then screamed again as another one was biting into his dick, and another one was jumping from his collarbone right at his eyes… and he frantically slapped the dick biter off and now the other one was hanging precariously from his lower right eyelid so he snapped his head and it flipped keening away. . . .

He stumbled back, kicking at them, sending five of the miniature Lisses flying, head over heels. Something bit his left ankle and he shook it loose and then stamped on it so it squealed with pain.

He shouted at the fabber, *"Shut down!"* But it ignored him, over-ridden by Liss, and he saw it was printing a big, muscular flesh-colored boa constrictor, which oozed out of the chute as if it had been waiting in there. A pink boa—but it had Liss's hate-disfigured face, which was jabbering, something about *"Your life will be rammed the way you smashed mine…"*

Then four more of the little homunculi raced around him and jumped on his legs from the back and he shrieked like scared tot and spun around to shake them off, slapping at himself. Something was perched on his shoulder, a tiny voice hissing in his ear: "You shall not know her in the meat, you shall not touch her! I'll die to stop it!"

"Moron!" Lucius yelled, yanking the thing from his ear and then throwing it. "She's just a trendy little bitch sucking at my old man's money!"

Then Lucius saw the pink man-flesh snake winding sinuously across the floor toward him, its every motion conveying its intention. Lucius turned and ran into the hall yelling *"Close and stay shut!"* at the door. It slammed shut and he ran down the hall—and skidded to a stop, feeling a piercing pain in the center of his back.

One of the printer homunculi had gotten on him and was gnawing through his spine.

He yelled, *"Daaaad!"* as he spun around and smashed his back against the wall. He felt the Liss-thing splatter apart but—a little too late. His legs went limp and he was on his face. It had eaten right through his spine. He'd have to get a nerve-grow to get his legs back.

Lucius crawled down the hall, pulling himself along, gnashing his teeth. He got to his studio, and shouted at his personal comm, "Get me Lew Schooner! Quick! Emergency! Life and death!"

The call went through—as they rarely did on the first try—and his dad was ogling down at him from the holobox. "What the fuck, Lucius! You've got blood all over you!"

"I've been attacked, my fabber was bio-hacked! It's Kriss Liss! He's the one that broke into that behavioral biohack! Turn him in, tell them he's attacking people with that shit, tell them—"

That's when he heard the crashing from down the hall, and he turned his head and said, "Dad, oh shit— send help! There's a thing, it's like a—"

But then it was slithering in to the room, and in two seconds it was winding around him and squeezing, and squeezing *harder*, and his dad was cursing and shouting at someone to get Sterly Breeson on the line and—

And then blood gushed from Lucius's mouth. But it was the splintering of his ribcage that killed him.

3

Kriss had to shoot her bodyguard to get in, and the feds were only minutes away so he had to get everything done fast. The door to Annabel Lee's veer room was ajar and there she was, she really *was*, in person, lying on the VR couch under the projector that sent the signals to her brain and she was smiling and muttering like a person in a dream...

And she was lovely.

He stood beside her couch and said, "You know what an exploding ant is, Annabel? *Colobopsis explodens*—entomology is my hobby. These ants sacrifice themselves to kill their enemies, by grasping them and exploding. A biological suicide bomber."

"I think someone's in my room," she said dreamily. "I better call the police and switch off—"

"Police and feds are coming, no need to call them, my loe," he said, as he took off his clothes. "I've done a biohack on myself. You set me against Lucius and now he's dead but he turned me in and I'm not going to let them take me and no one can take you but me, so..."

He threw himself onto her. And with the new biohack he'd introduced into the very cells of his body. . . .

Kriss exploded. His bones were shrapnel. Annabel screamed as she died. He hadn't time to scream, himself.

But he managed a smile as his head spun across the room.

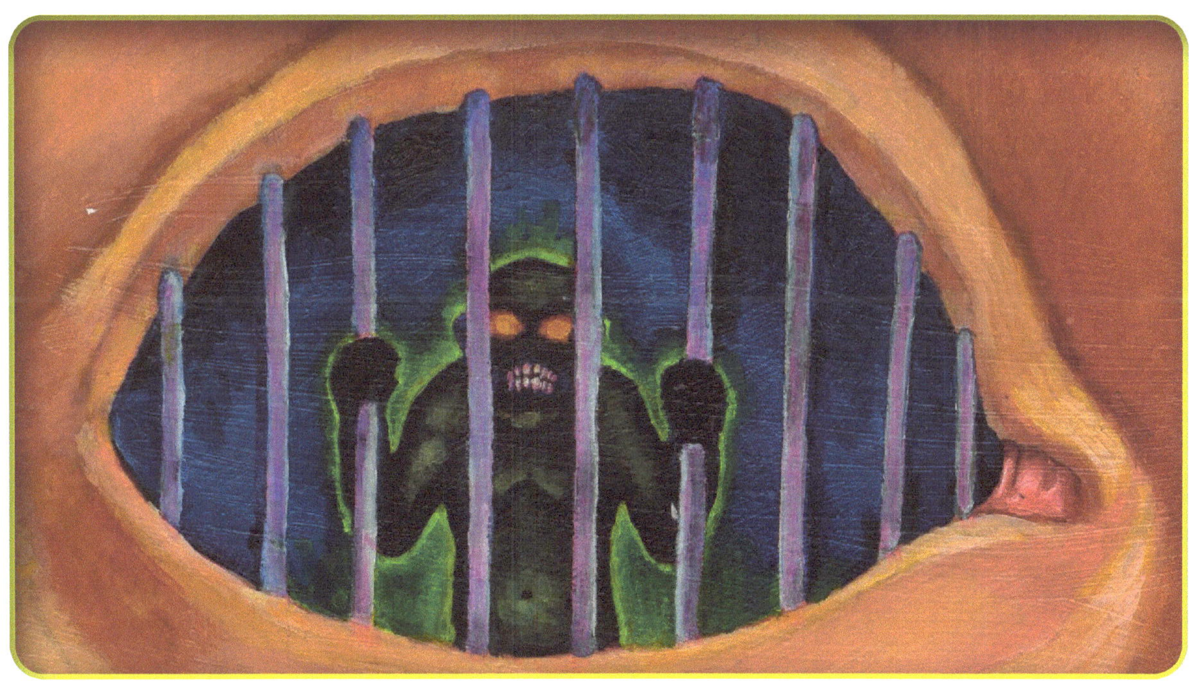

CURSE OF THE DEAD CENTER

JOHN WAYNE COMUNALE

"Cursed." The man's voice was loud but nonchalant. "Whole place is cursed."

Terry could hear them shout before getting out of his truck.

"Grounds' cursed too, don't waste your time."

In all the years Terry Sullivan had been a developer he hadn't had near as much trouble with a property as he had with this one. At a glance, it was a partially standing burned out shack sitting at an odd angle to the ground, which was on account of it having halfway sunk into a massive hole beneath. The opening was lined with jagged edges of charred wood and busted cement, deterrents from the twisted black mess below where the fire had been its angriest.

It used to be a club, a rock club, or more appropriately a *punk* rock club. At least at the end it was. Places like *The Dead Center* usually take a while to get on their feet and find their iden-

tity, only it seemed to find it faster than most. It started as a dirty beer bar with a small stage in the corner graced mostly by wannabe singer/songwriters with too much moxie and too little talent. The only standout in the bunch was a kid who went by Tony Fink.

He couldn't sing or play guitar well at all, not at first. Some say he never did, but they were jealous. He had passion and grit; two things painfully absent from others attempting to launch their star from the same triangular shaped platform in the dark corner of that bar.

He called himself *That Finkelstein Shit Kid* when it was just him, a nod to a movie most people listening to his music hadn't seen but still amused by the wordplay. When he put the band together, the name changed briefly to *Those Finkelstein Shit Kids,* and then to *Those Shit Kids* before settling simply on *Shit Kids.* They were always billed as *Tony Fink and the Shit Kids* though the name was never officially changed until after the fire, and even then, hardcore fans didn't recognize the modification. It would always be *Shit Kids* to them.

This wasn't the kind of thing Terry was interested in. He couldn't give a shit less about some shitty band's legacy or whatever their handful of trashy braindead 'fans' had to say about them. He wanted to make his money and move on, but he couldn't do that with Tony Fink's supporters refusing to leave the property.

This was the last time he was coming out here to talk though, this was the last conversation before the police were brought in to remove them forcibly. Terry didn't want it to come to that, he didn't want there to be a scene. This was why he headed straight for the person who had some semblance of control over the group, the one they would listen to.

Tony's brother, Frank, was sitting in his usual spot six feet to the right of the hole. His portable canvas camping chair had seen better days, and from the looks of Frank, so had he. The bottom half of his belly hung like a waxing crescent moon from the bottom of his ill-fitting *Shit Kids* shirt. His hair was an unkempt wild tangle of brush atop his head and clutched in his right hand was a tall can of Pabst Blue Ribbon beer. A small Styrofoam cooler with more of the same sat on the ground next to him.

This wasn't his first encounter with Frank who was in fact who filled him in on the story of Tony and *The Dead Center*. He referred to it as *The Dead* though along with the other creepy fans who skulked the property day and night like it was their job to keep people from getting in, or something else from getting out. They were hard to communicate with them because they spoke mostly in broken sentences peppered liberally with lyrics from *Shit Kids* songs, but Terry felt like he a good chance of getting through to Frank.

"Cursed," Frank said when Terry was within ten feet of the hole. "Place is cursed. Best just to move along."

"Hey there, Frank," Terry said approaching Frank's chair, his throne. "I know about the curse.

You told me remember? It's me Terry. You told me the whole story about a week ago about your brother and . . . this place."

Frank stared and said nothing as he swigged from the can of beer showing no sign of recognition toward the developer. Terry waited another moment, but Frank just drank again, deeply this time tipping the can up until it was empty. He tossed it into the hole and reached down for another from the cooler.

"So, you know then," he said pulling the tab on his fresh PBR. "Good."

"Yeah, good," Terry said burying his hands in his pockets, kicking at the dirt. "And I'm sorry about your brother Frank, really sorry. I know how it hurts to lose someone so close to you."

It was a lie. Terry had never lost anyone close to him.

"Thing is," he continued, "we all have to move on sometime, and I hate to say it, but I think it's that time for you and your . . . friends."

Terry gestured to the small clusters of people posted at different spots around the property in canvas chairs of their own, beers in hand. Frank looked confused, then hurt before his eyes showed the emotion they expressed best, anger.

"We can't," Frank replied simply and sipped his beer again. "We can't *move on*. We can't leave and you can't stay. The cur—"

"Yeah, yeah, the curse. I know." Terry was pacing now trying to keep his frustration from showing. "You told me, but the thing is this property has been bought by my company and we need to start working. I promise we'll be respectful to the memory of your brother. Maybe we can have a plaque put up or some—"

"Is this a joke to you?" Frank was standing now; his fresh beer lay on its side by the chair spilling into the dirt and grass. "Do you think we made this up? That we're *crazy* or something?"

"Now Frank, I didn't mean to imp—"

"Do you understand what a curse is? How it works? He cursed us. He cursed us all, this whole place!"

"*Who* cursed you?"

FORBIDDEN FUTURES 11
TOZIERS
DEAD
AN
BORN TO BE
BLACK
SABBATH!
AC DC

Terry regretted asking the moment the question left his mouth but thought allowing Frank to explain might deescalate the situation.

"Tony," Frank said. "My brother. He couldn't leave well enough alone, couldn't just be satisfied. He had to push it. He wanted more and he got it. Now, we're all paying the price."

This was the first time it occurred to Terry these people could *actually* be dangerous. It was evident whatever the curse was about, they believed in it whole heartedly. Frank's vehemence was intimidating.

"That music, *his* music he called it. It all started with that." Frank was rocking side to side now but didn't break eye contact with the developer. "He said he owed his success to the sacrifices he'd made and not the kind you think. But he needed more. Always more and more sacrifices. He was out of control."

"Sacrifices?"

"They were for whoever he'd gone into business with, his 'partner' he called them, only they were calling more of the shots than Tony. I loved my brother too much to let it keep going on. That's why we had the fire."

"Wait, wait," Terry stumbled. "Are you saying *you* started the fire that burned the club down and . . . killed your brother."

"It was less about killing him and more about stopping *it*, what he was becoming. We had to trap it to save Tony. It was the only thing we could do at that point."

Frank stooped to pluck another beer from the cooler and, feeling their eyes on him, Terry turned to find everyone on the property intently watching him. Beers in hand, silent, staring. Something wasn't right. His truck was parked fifty feet away but might as well have been fifty miles. He fought an overwhelming urge to run, to sprint to the truck, take off, and let the cops deal with this mess of crazies.

The sea of cold blank stares operated like a barrier that kept him from acting on the impulse. He didn't think they'd let him get too far.

"Look, Frank," Terry started. "I think this is just a misunderstanding. I'm going to go back and talk with my bosses to see if we can do some—"

"The only bad thing to come out of the whole mess was the curse. Son-of-a-bitch got it out at the last possible second. Otherwise, we wouldn't be having this conversation."

Terry took a step back. He didn't like the way Frank spoke now, his tone and inflection had gone dark. What was he thinking coming out here by himself to try and persuade a group of burnout psycho-squatters to 'kindly move along'? He should've called the police from the start. Too bad should'ves don't mean shit when it's already too late.

"Frank, I want you to—"

"We are though," Frank continued. "Having this conversation, I mean. It's unfortunate but nothing we can do about it now. We just have to keep it going so Tony stays safe, so *it* doesn't get out."

He gestured over his shoulder to the hole behind him, and Terry took another step back.

"So, you see, we can't leave. We're bound by responsibility. It's our duty. If we fail, none of what Tony did matters anymore, and he gave too much for that to happen. The sacrifices must continue. For Tony. For the *Shit Kids*."

Terry turned to run but was stopped by a wall of Tony's dirty faithful, all of whom were now standing directly behind him blocking his route of escape. Their dead eyes fixed into malevolent stares rimmed in a dull orange glow. Somewhere in the background over their heads he saw the flames. His truck was on fire.

He spun back around and found Frank had closed the gap between them. It happened fast. Terry was already falling before he realized Frank had grabbed his arm and flung him toward the gaping burned-out maw, the hole his brother died in. No, the hole he *killed* his brother in.

It was where the curse started and as Terry fell face first hurling toward scorched remains of what equated to love and death, he understood.

WE ARE LESION FOR WE ARE MANY

by Cullen Bunn

Every morning, Isaac stands at his apartment window, sipping coffee from his favorite mug as he watches the world go by. He spies upon the people hurrying along the sidewalk, brushing past one another, clutching paper sacks full of bagels or greasy breakfast sandwiches, briefcases in hand or backpacks slung over shoulders, on their way to high-paying careers and dead-end jobs in equal measure. Some keep their heads down, avoiding eye contact with those they pass. Others hold phones to their ears, showing those around them that they are having "very important conversations" that "must not be interrupted." Still others have their ears plugged up with buds, and they bob their heads as they listen to their tunes.

Hustle and bustle and mind-your-own-fucking business.

This is how Isaac likes to start his day.

It reminds him that we're all part of the same machine, businessmen in their three-piece suits, single moms in their fast food uniforms, the homeless guy who clutches a handout cup but doesn't bother asking for change because he knows no one gives a shit. Isaac himself, standing at the window four stories up, observing the crowd, morning after morning, expecting something—

Different.

A man staggers down the street. He wears an athletic track suit darkened with wet blood. He is pale. Sweating. His stomach—the actual, glistening, purple-grey organ—emerges from his belly button, tethered to him by a tangle of veins, floating beside him, bobbing in the air like a helium-filled balloon.

At first, other pedestrians don't notice the man—because they are actively trying *not* to notice him.

Or they don't realize what is happening.

Or they don't care.

Finally, someone pays attention. A woman in a business suit spots the man. He clutches at her, pleading for help, his disembodied stomach drifting in the air. She screams. Isaac can't hear her, not from his fourth-floor window, but he can see the horror on her face. She is being accosted by a man with his insides on his outside.

Of course, she screams.

Others take note. Many of them scream, too. The combined cacophony of their startled fright *is* enough to reach Isaac's window. Collectively aghast, the crowd recoils from the afflicted man.

"Cess?" Isaac calls over his shoulder. "Come here. Something weird is happening outside."

Below, the crowd scatters in all directions, all save the man and his floating stomach. He stands perfectly still now, no longer in a panic, no longer pleading for help. His head tilts back. He looks toward the sky. It seems almost as if he is looking straight back at Isaac.

Isaac steps back from the window.

"Cess, you've got to see this."

Cecily doesn't answer.

Isaac hurries to the bedroom door, throwing it open. "There's a guy out here with—"

Cecily, his girlfriend of four years, stands statue-like, head tilted back. A halo of spattered blood stains the carpet around her. From her bloodied mouth, a hovering cascade of organs—her heart and lungs, a tangle of connective tendrils—emerges, slowly undulating in the air above her.

Sour bile rises in Isaac's throat.

Tears burn his eyes.

His head spins.

Leaving Cess behind, he returns to the kitchen, where his cell phone lies in a pile along with his keys and wallet and a few crumpled bills. With twitching fingers, he grabs his phone, punching in 9-9...

No, that's not right.

1-1-9...

His fingers refuse to cooperate.

He clenches his hand into a sweaty fist, squeezes them tight, flexes them.

His chest heaves.

His stomach churns.

He wonders if what has happened to Cecily, if what has happened to the man on the street below, is happening to him. Will his heart and lungs, will his stomach...

...his liver...

...kidneys...

...intestines...

…erupt from his body to float, churning and oozing, in the air around him?

His fingers dance across the phone screen, this time finding the right numbers in the right order.

"We're sorry," the inhuman… fleshless… voice on the other end of the line tells him. "All circuits are busy at this time."

"Fuck!"

In instinctive frustration, he throws the phone across the room. It strikes the fridge and bounces to the floor.

A voice speaks behind him.

"Be not afraid."

"Cess?" he whispers, but he doesn't yet turn around.

"Be not afraid."

It is definitely his girlfriend's voice, or at least a gargling, garbled mockery of her voice, as if she is speaking with her mouth full.

Full of her own viscera.

Legs quivering, Isaac faces her.

Cess stands just outside the bedroom. Her head is still tilted back, her heart and lungs still suspended over her, slipping and sliding across the door frame, leaving a smear of glistening red. Bloody drool drips down her chin.

"Be not afraid," she gurgles, "for this has always been our purpose."

Isaac bolts for the front door, hurls it open, and almost falls out into the hall. A long, undulating wail escapes his throat, following him. Following him the way the floating organs follow the man on the street below, the way they follow Cess. His legs feel like they might give out as he races toward the elevator at the end of the hallway.

From other apartments, he hears panicked cries, terrified shrieks, and gurgling gasps. A pool of blood oozes from under one of the doors. Another door is open an inch or two, and as Isaac glimpses something lashing about, tendrils of meat whipping wetly through the room beyond.

Cess shuffles out of the still-open door to the apartment.

"Be not afraid."

At the end of the hall, Isaac rapidly taps the elevator's call button. He glances back, sees his girlfriend slowly walking toward him. A bell rings and the doors slide open. He lunges inside and hits the "Lobby" button.

As the doors close, Isaac watches Cess shambling down the hall, following after him in a meandering gait. Her heart and lungs…

…the heart still pulsing…

…the lungs still inflating and deflating…

…bob in the air above her.

And Isaac realizes she is still alive.

The elevator descends.

At the second floor, the elevator lurches to a stop. The doors open. Three more people shuffle inside, pressing in close to Isaac, pushing him back. Two men and a woman. Neighbors in the building. Isaac recognizes them though he has never exchanged more than a few in-passing pleasantries with them.

One of the men glistens wetly. He is naked, save for a towel around his waist. His nipples puff open, like flowers of meat, and one of his lungs emerges from each, floating.

The other man is dressed for work. A suit and tie. No shoes, though. His pants are soaked in gore. An organ—his liver, maybe—rises out from under the seat of his pants, from his anus most likely. It is dark and diseased, speckled with fibrous yellow patches and polyps.

The woman clutches feebly at her face with twitching fingers. An involuntary movement. Her brain has oozed out from one of her eye sockets, and it hovers above her. Her eye drips down her cheek from a cluster of nerves.

Isaac gags as they move in around him, the wet tendrils of veins and muscle slithering dangerously close to him.

The woman turns, jerkily, toward him. Her loose, goggling eyeball stares at him.

"Be not afraid," she says. "This is our purpose, fulfilled at last."

It's the longest conversation he's ever had with her.

The elevator opens once more. Lobby. And Isaac's companions shuffle out, ignoring him. Panting, trying to catch his breath, Isaac waits for a moment, back pressed against the wall. The doors start to slide closed again, someone upstairs summoning the elevator. Isaac slips out.

He is met by several more people—other victims—surrounded by floating organs. Shuffling, moving toward the doors, toward the street, their exposed hearts and stomachs and brains and kidneys and livers bumping and thumping along the ceilings and walls.

A young man, dressed in the attire of a bike messenger, cowers in a corner, crouched down. He clutches at his head as he snivels and weeps.

"This isn't happening. This isn't happening. This isn't happening."

Isaac considers approaching the man, speaking to him, but stops himself.

What would he say?

What comfort could he offer?

Words almost slip past his lips.

Be not afraid.

He thinks he's going to puke.

If he pukes, though, what else comes up with his coffee and the bit of toast he had for breakfast? Will his innards boil out of his mouth and nose? Will vomit-flecked organs float above him like a fleshy cloud?

He rushes outside.

A crowd has formed again. More of the victims, standing still and looking to the sky, gather in the street. Their organs blossom from mouths and nostrils, from ears and nipples, from eyes and belly buttons. Floating overhead, they almost resemble weird, meaty bonsai trees. Those who stagger out of the apartment building, out of all the buildings lining the street, fall still, as if made vestigial by the fresh air.

There are others, too, like Isaac, who are not afflicted by this bizarre...

...illness?

That's what this must be, Isaac thinks, a disease causing the body to reject its own organs.

Afflicted.

The term cements in Isaac's mind.

The *un*afflicted stagger past the "meat tree humans," bewildered, afraid to touch them, unable to look away as they try to puzzle out exactly what is happening.

Meat tree humans.

Others try to snap the victims out of it, grabbing them by the shoulders and shaking them, clutching at their arms and urging them to come back inside.

And what good would that do?

Would their lungs and hearts and intestines and stomachs just slither back inside their bodies, like snails retreating into their shells?

Others wail in horror or weep in desperation.

"This is the end!"

"Judgment!"

"Oh, God! There's more of them!"

Still others, laughing nervously to themselves, use their phones to take pictures.

More of the afflicted shuffle out of the apartment building. Cecily is among them. Once they reach the street, once they reach the morning light, they stop walking and look to the sky.

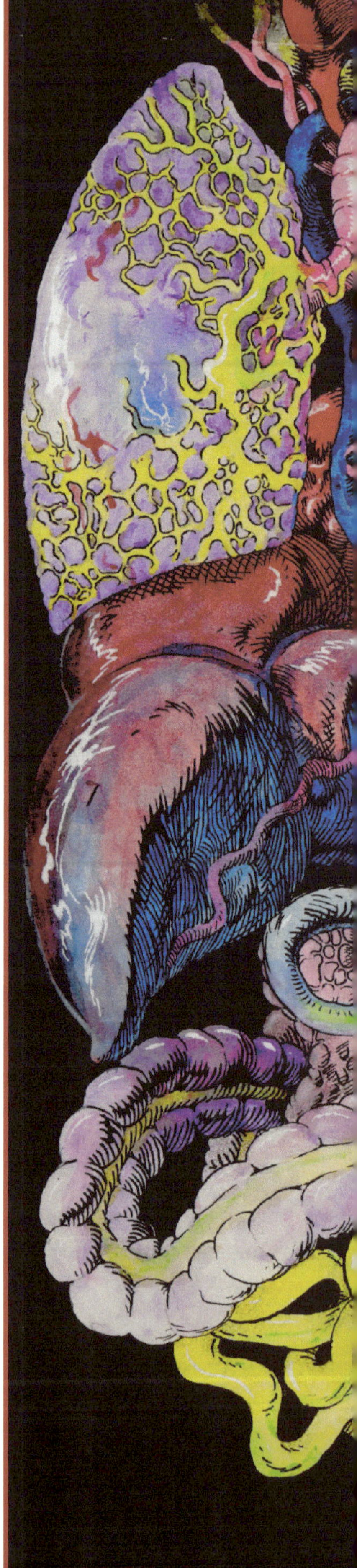

A hush falls across the crowd.

Even the frantic, pleading prayers fall silent.

Only for a moment, though.

"Be not afraid." The meat tree humans speak as one. "This is our purpose, fulfilled at last. The seed was planted long ago, and now the time of harvest is here."

A gasp rises from the crowd.

The afflicted *float*.

They rise off the ground, carried aloft by their hovering organs. The fleshy tendrils pull taut with the weight. The afflicted almost look like they are doing a back-float in mid-air.

Blood showers down, spatters across the faces of the onlookers.

"It's the rapture," someone mutters.

"Take me with you!" someone cries.

And "I've been good!"

And "Take my intestines!"

And "You can have my spleen!"

And "I don't need my heart!"

Some of the onlookers charge the floating bodies, leaping at them, grabbing at them, trying to pull them down.

"Don't let the aliens take you!"

Isaac watches as the undiseased, the whole, the unafflicted masses leap and grab at the rising bodies. Most of the floating figures are out of reach already, but some are close enough to grab a foot or a hand, a leg.

"Stay with us!"

A man grabs hold of Cess, his hand wrapping around her ankle, and he tugs her down. Another man joins him. A woman. They drag her back toward the earth.

"Hey!" Isaac yells. "What are you doing?"

They grab at the heart and lungs that rise from her bloodied mouth. They tear at them, ripping them free. The tendrils of flesh lash around wildly, wounded, spurting weird fluids and blood. The attackers rush off, almost dancing, carrying the heart and lungs above their heads, a joyous prize, letting the fluids spatter down upon them. Cess spasms and twitches on the ground, then falls still.

Rushing to her side, Isaac clutches at her, but she's cold and unmoving, the light gone from her eyes.

Cecily's attackers—her murderers—prance with their fleshy, pulsing, puss-and-blood spurting trophy through the crowd.

The heart beats.

The lungs breathe.

She's not dead, Isaac realizes.

He charges the attackers, tackles the man who holds the heart and lungs. They crash to the ground, tumbling over one another. Isaac drives his fist into the man's face.

"Let her go!"

The man's nose crumples.

"Let her go!"

His teeth break, sheared off at the roots.

The jagged, broken edges dig into Isaac's knuckles.

The other attackers try to pull Isaac away, but he strikes and them, battering the woman across the nose, elbowing the man in the throat.

He yanks Cecily's organs away from the man. The man's fingers dig into the flesh, tear at it, but Isaac clambers to his feet, kicks the man in the balls. The man releases the organs. Isaac grabs them and pulls them close to his chest, feels them beating against him, feels the warmth of the spurting blood.

Others are looking at him in shock.

In horror.

In anger.

With covetous eyes.

Isaac runs, holding his girlfriend's organs close, his feet splashing in the blood lapping across the street, as all around, the bodies of the meat tree humans rise toward the heavens.

It takes only a few weeks for a new religion— the Rapture of Flesh—to take shape.

Health nuts meet religious zealots.

We are flesh. We are the whole of our parts. We await the moment of elation when our parts will sweep us to Heaven. We must care for our bodies so that we can achieve paradise.

They wage war against fast food chains.

The burger joints and taco stands and pizza delivery services join forces, create their own faith, claiming that the grease and sugars only emboldens and strengthens the flesh for the journey to Heaven.

The war is vicious and cruel.

Bombings at burger joints.

Deadly drive-by pizza deliveries.

Butchery in the name of faith in one month.

There are those, of course, those who believe religion has nothing to do with what has happened.

Their organs are harvested in supplication.

Human sacrifice in six weeks.

It's not long before the elitists rise to power.

Which organ is most important? The heart? The brain? The stomach? The kidneys?

"It is my brain that will be chosen," claims one priest, "for I have cultivated an understanding of philosophy and art."

"It is my heart," claims another, "because I love my fellow man."

"It is my stomach because I have strengthened it with fried chicken and pizza rolls."

Eight weeks until bloody dissent within the churches.

Isaac seeks a safe place.

He knows he must keep Cecily's organs hidden.

If others were to discover the secrets she held, they would kill him and take her from him. Every morning, Isaac stands on the front porch, and he looks out across the forest that surrounds the little cabin. There are no people, not out here in the wilderness. There is no coffee, either, which is more tragic.

He clutches Cecily's heart and lungs close, feeling the sluggish pulse, feeling the unyielding pull from the unseen force above. If he were to release his hold, the organs would levitate off into space. When he's not holding her close, he ties the cold, flaccid tendrils to a bed post in the cabin so he can get a few restless moments of sleep.

When I wake, I might have my organs rising out of my ass.

He found the mountain hideaway two weeks ago. Pre-fabbed log cabin. Two corpses, one without a brain, the other without kidneys, were sprawled out front. The previous owners. They wouldn't mind Isaac squatting in the cabin, away from everyone, for a while.

He had buried the bodies—the leftovers, he mused to himself—in the yard.

All is quiet.

The air smells like old bandages in need of changing.

Cecily's lungs turn grey within a week.

Her heart turns black.

Bits of flesh flake off like ashes.

The spoiled meat smell is nauseating.

And yet the organs continue to work.

She continues to live.

She communicates.

Tiny ulcerating sores suction open across the meat of her heart and lungs. Oozing thick, milky spittle, they open and close, like tiny, eager mouths. They speak in whispers. The voice is Cecily's.

"You should have allowed me to ascend."

"I didn't understand," Isaac says. "I didn't realize what was happening."

"This is our purpose. This is why we were seeded into the flesh of this world so long ago, when humans were new. We await the moment when we are called home, when we can join the collective, when we might become something new."

"I was afraid."

"There is no fear in the collective. There is only peace. There is only unity. Thousands of lives from thousands of worlds, thousands of universes, all merged and fused together in endless peace."

"Why weren't we all chosen?"

"The building of new life takes time. There must be an orderly ascension. Your time will come. Be not afraid."

"This is but the temptation of the flesh. Peace awaits. Unity. Togetherness."

"We're together now."

"This is a lie. I do not belong here. I must be free to join the collective."

"But I'll be alone."

"Only for a short time. The ascension will claim you in time. We will be made whole once more. This is our purpose."

"I don't understand."

"You are but the host. How could you comprehend the truth? We have been summoned. The collective calls to us, as it has called to countless other worlds. When your time comes, do not resist."

"Are you in pain?"

"I cannot exist for much longer without ascension."

"I'm sorry. I never meant to hurt you."

"Fear not."

Slowly, hesitantly, Isaac opens his arms. Cecily's organs slip from his grasp. Bobbing like partially-deflated balloons, they rise towards the heavens.

Toward blissful unity.

Toward the promise of paradise.

Screeching, a hawk darts out of the trees, flying like a missile, snapping the heart and lungs from the air, tearing into them, digging its talons into the greying flesh. It swoops around, clutching the organs tight, then vanishes back into the forest to enjoy its meal in peace.

Isaac blinks.

The promise of eternal life, denied.

He sits there, staring into the vast, empty sky, through the blue, through the red, through the black.

Stars wink back at him.

A deer wobbles from the forest on spasming legs. Its fur is spattered with blood. From numerous sores, numerous oozing lesions on its body, organs emerge, floating, tethered by bloody tendrils of sinew.

Its stomach. Its heart. Its brain.

Other organs Isaac doesn't recognize.

Alien organs.

The deer cocks its head to the side.

"Be not afraid," it says.

Wearily, Isaac rises.

He goes inside.

He goes to bed.

And he says his prayers before he sleeps.

INVASION
INVASION OF THE BODY SNATCHERS
- BY -
Michael Dubisch
SPECIAL THANKS TO —
BILL TOWNSEND, TOM VINCENT,
MARIO BRUNO, STEVEN R.
BISSETTE & FRANK VURRARO.

BAM BAM BAM BAM
BAM BAM BRM BR
BAM BAM BRM B
BLORP!
SPLAT

BEEP — BEEP — BEEP — BEEP — BEEP — BEEP
SHIP BEING RECALLED. NO RESPONSE FROM PILOTS...
BEEP — BEEP — BEEP

BAM
BAM
BLAM
BRAM
RAM

HEART OF THE CITY

ERICA L. SATIFKA

You sling your pack over your shoulder as you thread your way along the long-abandoned subway tracks, tracing the old routes still somewhat legible within the flesh of the city-thing. The platform numbers are unreadable, buried beneath thin membranes, so you count them out silently.

Fucker was supposed to meet me here an hour ago, you think. You turn on your phone, but it doesn't help your visibility. That's the last time I use a dating app.

Suddenly, you hear the sloshing of footsteps behind you. You grip your pack tighter, even though there's nothing in there worth stealing. "Vinnie?" you manage to squeak out, though as soon as the beefy figure looms into view you know it's not your date.

"This way," she says.

You stay silent, hoping that she'll just think you're some kind of tumor the city-thing coughed up, but she doesn't fall for it. "I'm waiting for someone."

"Wouldn't advise screwing down here," she says. "The city don't like it."

Heat flushes your cheeks. "We weren't going to do that."

The musclebound woman gives you a lopsided grin, as if to say yeah, right. "So, you coming?"

You don't really want to follow this stranger, but you don't want to wait around in this maze of desiccated flesh either. You trail behind her and her battery-operated flashlight, which illuminates various sections of the city-thing: a rippled ridge of well-marbled meat that might have been a turnstile, an expanse of white fat that encrusts an entire platform like a chalk deposit. All this has lurked under your feet unseen for most of your life.

"Not too much farther," the guide says.

"Where are we going?" You wonder if it's the place Vinnie planned to take the two of you, his sick idea of a date. Now that you think about it, he probably did want to fuck you here, right on the dead city-thing.

The guide turns around. Her eyes look milky in the low light. Maybe she's just lived down here so long that she's turned colorless, like some kind of cave grub. "The city's not dead, you know. It's very much alive," she says, as if reading your thoughts.

"Doesn't seem like it."

"You'll see when we get there." You hear a smattering of voices beyond the next turn, and wherever this pushy woman is taking you, you know it has to be close.

The chamber ahead of you is awash in light, and you nearly collapse from the shock of entering that bright area from the near-darkness. You freeze, almost drop your pack. "Thanks, but I think —"

"We're all friends here," the guide says as she directs you to one of the bare spaces on the ground, which seems to be formed of the city-thing's spongy intestine. "Sit."

You look around at the others. People lived in these tunnels long before the advent of the city-thing, so it shouldn't be surprising that they still do, but you're a little surprised anyway. One of the former-subway-dwellers has a cook fire going, and that's how you know the guide has to be full of shit. No way would the city-thing let homeless people set fire to its carcass if it were alive.

"I said sit down," she says, and so you do. The material is almost comfortable enough to sleep on, and you pinch yourself awake to keep yourself from doing exactly that.

One of the men hands you a bowl of something sludgy and green. You push it around with a spoon to be polite.

On the other side of the chamber, two old men fight over a brightly-colored jacket. Even in the dim light of the flashlight, cook fire, and various electric lanterns, the jacket's familiar. You stand up, the bowl of rancid soup spilling at your feet, seeping into the rubbery floor of this place. "Let me see that!" The two men whirl around, and you feel yourself shrink. "Please?"

Neither makes a move to hand over the jacket, but the guide manages to wrest it away from them without effort. You gather she's something of an authority figure here. "What, you cold or something?"

You grab the item from her, inspecting the hand-sewn tag on the front. Vinnie. "He was here?"

"Oh, that's who you came here to see? Yeah, he was by." She shrugs. "Didn't make it."

All of a sudden, you don't care about anything except getting out. This was only supposed to be your third date anyway. You thumb your phone on again and move back toward the direction you came from.

"I think you could make it, though," she says. "I have a good feeling."

Against your better judgment, you swivel on your heel and stalk back to the guide. "Make what?"

"Make it past the city-thing," she says. "Earn its honor."

"And what do I get if I 'win'?"

"The truth."

You know the truth about the city-thing, or close enough. It appeared beneath Boston when you were seven years old. Like most, you'd ignored it, even as its silent presence hung over – or rather below – every interaction. This is the first time you've even seen it up close, and you could have gone the rest of your life without getting up close and personal with the dead alien slumbering beneath your hometown. "I want to see Vinnie's body. If you people haven't eaten it yet."

The guide laughs, her flashlight jittering. "We don't do that here. We do other things, but not that."

After forcing some of the vile soup down your throat—it tastes like boiled cauliflower in pork gravy, and for all you know that's what it is – the subway-dwellers take you to Vinnie. One of the men plays his electric lantern over your date's narrow face and you see that he's smiling. You hadn't been close to loving this guy, but you still feel a little bad for his family.

"How did he die?"

"He came for pleasure," the guide says, "and the city gave him what he wanted."

You search for her eyes in the murky dark. "So why do you think I'm here? It could kill me too."

"But it won't," she says, and you believe she believes she's telling the truth.

You take another long look at the bag of skin and organs that had once been Vinnie B. You realize, belatedly, that you'd never learned his last name. "So this test...?"

"Over here." You and the guide, and about a half-dozen of the subway-dwellers, move to an alcove not too far from Vinnie's perfectly preserved corpse. She throws her flashlight over a patch of the skin-wall, and the soup nearly rockets out of your belly when you see what's there.

A curtain of blond hair, behind which something twitches slow and methodical.

The guide draws the hair aside with one hand while training her flashlight with the other, and reveals a small gobbet of black flesh. You'd think it was a heart if not for the color. It wheezes as it beats. It doesn't look like it can pump more than a teaspoon of liquid, if that.

"That thing killed Vinnie," you say, not believing it for a second.

"Give it a pet," she says.

You step back, certain you don't want to go near that thing. "You first."

The guide doesn't hesitate as she reaches out and strokes one of the ventricles. A beatific expression alights on her grizzled face. It quite honestly looks like a spectacular experience, and if Vinnie saw one of the subway-dwellers do it before he arrived, it's no surprise that he decided to take the plunge.

You look down at your hands, which have grown cold and clammy in the depths of the city-thing's carcass. You have no desire to give that wretched thing behind the hair curtain a stroke, even with the guide's demonstration.

On the surface, in the depopulated remains of Boston, nobody ever discusses the city-thing. It had showed up one day, killing presumably everyone riding the subway at the time, and many more people besides. After the initial massacre, and resultant flight, things had gone on as they always had, a forced normalcy, a coerced and specific amnesia.

"Well?" says the guide, lingering radiance limning her broad face.

Why not? you think. After all, you'd been willing enough to explore this place only a few hours ago. You stretch out a finger and slide it down the main ridge of the city-thing's black shriveled heart.

There's an intake of air then, a great breath that feels strong enough to douse the cook fire. But you can't see if it does, because the malleable flesh of the alcove flows around you, isolating you within a slippery capsule. This is the test, and you can't tell whether or not you're passing. A great groan sounds from the putrid-looking organ in front of you, and then the city-thing begins to speak to you, not with words but with pictures that beam fully-formed into your silly head.

I arrived here on a cool clear morning.

I burrowed into the heart of your city, and died.

Your atmosphere was too harsh for me, too heavy.

These people nurtured me, brought me back, just a little.

I reward them with visions and good health.

Now I do the same for you, my friend.

You wake with the taste of the soup in your mouth, and begin to spit. Your eyes slam open, and you immediately search for your bearings. You're not in the alcove with the heart in it anymore, but nestled on a ridge of bone roughly approximating a spinal column.

"Oh, you're awake." It's one of the old men, one of the people who'd certainly lived here before the coming of the city-thing.

You stretch your limbs. It feels like you've been sleeping for days, and maybe you have. "Where's the guide? You know, the woman with the flashlight." You hadn't caught her name either.

He gestures at the place where you saw Vinnie all those hours or days ago. The guide is there next to him, her smile frozen in the same rictus, her body covered with a filmy layer of slime.

You look up at the high flesh walls and vaulted bony ceiling of the city-thing. "I thought the city liked her."

"She chose this," he says. He doesn't seem sad, and neither are you.

Inspecting the walls closer, you see they're moving just a bit, making the hair curtain rustle. It hadn't been doing that before. The city-thing's meal has rejuvenated it somehow. "So what do I do now? Can I go back to the surface?"

As you say this, you know that you will never go back to the surface.

"Bring more people. That's all it's ever wanted, some friends."

Another of the homeless men brings over your pack, and yet another claps the guide's flashlight into your palm. They gesture toward the endless tunnels housing thousands of pounds of not-quite-dead alien flesh.

You waver just a moment as you stand there on the intestine. You can't imagine that the city-thing's new localized breathing is doing is anything positive for the good few people left in Boston.

But something tells you that they aren't your people anymore. These are your people now, whether you like it or not.

You nod at the men, spit a last bit of soup-taste out of your mouth, and start walking.

It wants friends? you think.

I'll give it some friends.

The Ultimate! Modern!! Convenience!!!

By Nick Mamatas

Dick was so excited he spoke before swallowing his first mouthful of breakfast. "Omnipovac!" The triangle of toast fell to his plate; his hand smacked against the newspaper. To Lurlene it sounded like a made-up word. "Can you believe it!" Dick demanded to know of his wife.

"I'm sure I cannot," said Lurlene. She stuck out her tongue too, but Dick couldn't see, as he was a junior executive down at the Krafty Konfections Plant and Corporate HQ and so his daily paper was *The Courant,* a great drapery of a broadsheet. The newlyweds may have well been eating breakfast in separate rooms. "A vacuum cleaner with all-powerful suction?" she asked.

"Don't even think about it, darling," said Dick. "I'm already making payments on the Frigidaire, the radar range, the Mr. Coffee, the Dr. Crème Soda, the Recipe Rolodex and Foodstuff Filofax, the Hula Hoop Beautisizer—it's been working a charm, by the way, beautiful!—the wet bar in the cabana…

"And all the…feed," Dick said. The kitchen cabinets rattled, "But no, the Omnipovac isn't a household gadget for the lady of the house, greedy girl. It's an electronic brain!"

"Oh my," said Lurlene. She picked up the pep pill on her plate and sucked it between her lips. "How wonderful…or dreadful?"

That made Dick finally put down his paper. He folded it on his lap, glanced down at the slightly runny eggs Benedict for a moment, then for a second moment to register his displeasure, then met his wife's gaze. "Dreadful," he said plainly. "Do you understand what the existence of an electronic brain, one that a company can purchase, means for me? Means for us?"

Maybe Lurlene shouldn't have eaten her pep pill. The passivity pill was still right there on her plate. She needed the extra energy to handle the household chores while Dick was at work, but sometimes too much pep caused problems. "I'm sure I don't know, dear. Will you be wheeling an electronic brain in here to explain it to li'l ol' me? Shall I set another place? Will the electronic brain eat *its* eggs Benedict without being such a sour puss?"

"An electronic brain," Dick said through clenched teeth, "could mean the end of my job. Imagine it, Lurlene! A box of wires and vacuum tubes, an adding machine that can solve a thousand math problems a minute, and is never ever wrong. It never takes a day off, never demands a raise, never cheats at golf—"

"The Omnipovac plays golf?"

"No!" Dick snapped. Lurlene cackled, then quickly covered her mouth with her napkin, sending the utensils nested in it clattering across the linoleum floor. She giggled at that. The kitchen cabinets rattled again. It was five minutes till nine o'clock, and the chime sounded.

"Dang it, Lurlene. I must go," Dick said. He jabbed at his egg with his fork, and shoved what the tines had snagged into his mouth. "Omnipovac doesn't eat the doughnuts in the canteen for his breakfast either, but I guess today I will."

"Poor Dick," Lurlene said. "My poor Dick." She stood up and trailed Dick to the door and managed to brush her lips against the rear of his collar. He ran out to the driveway, slid into his Cadillac-V4 Rokit, eased out onto the street, and hit the scramjet. Four minutes across town, if the school crossing guard was nimble. The whole house shook. The kitchen cabinets burst open and out poured the gremlins.

Lurlene had no time to sigh. The feedbags, and a great kitchen knife, were at the door, since Lurlene couldn't carry the bags very far and Dick always had an attack of his old war wound when she asked him to do it. She expertly slit the bags, and gave each a kick, sending kibble tumbling out onto the FerevrWear wall-to-wall carpet. Off-ivory, her favorite color. The gremlins swarmed the feed, or most of them did. A couple got into the toaster, which immediately exploded. The pep pill was working great—Lurlene could go five minutes straight without blinking. She planted her back against the front door and held the knife out before her, her hand trembling. These gremlins, another souvenir of Dick's service in World War Quick, could get rambunctious!

They had names, the gremlins, your basic everyday British names. Dick had christened them all while they were still in their shells, writing the names of the RAF officers he worked with during the war right on the calcium carbonate. James, George, Charlie, Danny, Willie, and more, but the gremlins didn't answer to these names, or to anything but Dick's afterwork barking. Lurlene had to play it smart. Feint with the knife in her right hand, then kick with her left foot. Good thing she always wore heels to breakfast. Lurlene didn't belong the curlers and housedress set, no sirree.

Charlie got on the ceiling fan. Lurlene reached out and cranked the knob, sending the blades spinning. Bad move. With perfect timing, Charlie rode the fan for three rotations and then let go, sending himself flying right at Lurlene. She ducked, threw her forearms over her face…and didn't see Danny and some other gremlin—Alfie?—outflank her on both sides. They took her down. She ate a mouthful of FerevrWear fibres. Charlie smacked against the front door, and slid down it, squeaking slimily all the way, and landed on Lurlene's rump.

Lurlene planted her hands on the floor, just as Jock Roidman instructed at two o'clock every afternoon on the television, and pushed up. Charlie tried to ride her, but with quick shake of her hips, Lurlene sent him flying into a feedbag. She almost got up to her feet, but Willie and George looked up from their breakfasts and, mouths full of kibble, rushed he and got her by the legs. Lurlene was hoist into the air like she'd just been declared Mrs. Buttery Complexion at the Windham County Fair and Agritechnical Exposition. Gremlin hands found strange places. "*Dick!*" Lurlene cried out. His name was a useless, futile thing to wail. It was Dick who had smuggled the gremlins across the Atlantic after the war; Dick who named them; Dick who presented Lurlene with a Sewtite Semi-Automatic SuperLoom and bade her make little outfits for them; Dick who stayed up past midnight hunched over the Nadir Two-Tube Zortwave radio tuning in to one transdimensional station after another to conduct croaking, ululating sing-alongs with them till dawn; Dick who pilfered Lurlene's pep pills, ground them into powder, and snorted the dust off a fine black slab of obsidian with these little beasts whom he called his sweet sweet boys, Dick Dick Dick who…

Dick, who behind the wheel of Rokit, crashed right through the wall and barreled into the living room. Gremlins were fast. Willie tossed Lurlene into the air and met the vehicle's aerodynamic grille face-first. He cracked like a pineapple filled with black ink. The other gremlins scattered more successfully; poor Charlie, just happy to be here, scuttled under a lampshade.

Lurlene didn't see her life flash before her eyes. She didn't see the flashing rotors of the ceiling fan promising her a new hairdo. She blinked. And when her eyes opened, she was in her husband's arms. He smiled a bloodied, newly toothless smile at her. "Gotcha, darlin'!"

"Dick…" Lurlene said, "Oh, Dick. What brings you, uhm, home at this early hour."

"Laid off! he roared. "Kicked in the keister! Sacked, made redundant like my old friends might say."

"Was it Omnipovac?" Lurlene asked. She twisted a bit in his arms, trying to find a way to give him a consoling hug without mussing her hair or getting blood all over her exceptional new blouse. Everything smelled of steam and ozone.

"It was Omnipovac," Dick said. "An immortal thinking machine, programmed to make us choke on chocolate and wring every last penny out of the world. The boss announced that 'the economy has been solved', and so Omnipovac fired everyone. And I do mean fired—I barely made it out alive. Thankfully, I'm an ace pilot. Right, boys?" The gremlins cheered in their flatulent fashion. "You should have seen me, Lurlene! Serpentine, U-turn, full-speed reverse, J-turn, hit the afterburners, then the parachute. Omnipovac didn't know where to aim! The rest of the Krafty Konfections bowling team wasn't so lucky, I'm sorry to report. God rest their souls."

"Oh heavens! How awful. Whatever will we do for money? I mean…" Lurlene shot a look over Dick's shoulder. "We'll need to remodel, and in a hurry I'm afraid. Telstar says it's to rain tonight, and tornadoes all weekend. I fear for my rose bushes, Dick, and the FereveWear. It's not meant to be exposed to open air; the shag will start outgassing."

"Thirty-nine percent arsenic," yes," Dick said. "The safest wall-to-wall carpet on the market, but still. And we have another seven hundred mortgage payments. But never fear, my dear, my darling, my pretty doll, my pharmalogical lovetoy, your husband has a plan."

"Is it…" Lurlene licked her lips, imagining. "Is it opening a business of your own? You're the best candy butcher in the prefecture. And…" she hesitated as she glanced around at the ruins of her living room, the gremlins here and there eating kibble like they were bonbons, the steaming hulk of the V4 and the worrisome glow spilling from its atomic batteries, "perhaps the gremlins can work the assembly line."

"Oh, my plans involve factories and the boys, all right," Dick said, darkly. "But *not* making money!" Lurlene gasped. He couldn't mean it. The neighbors were gathering on the lawn. She reached out to cover his mouth, but he grabbed her wrist. "My plan" he announced, "is COMMUNISM!"

The gremlins cheered and danced about as Lurlene swooned at Dick's feet. In the corner, Charlie trembled in anticipation, the lampshade rattling on his head.

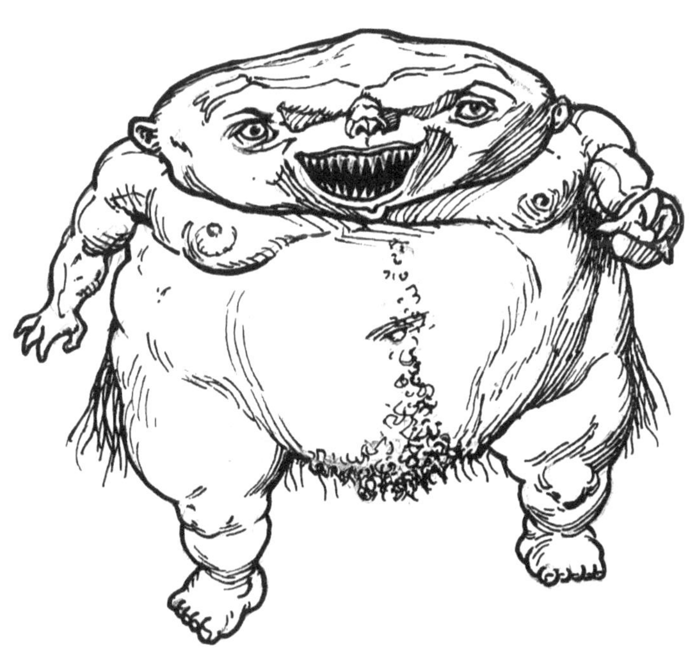

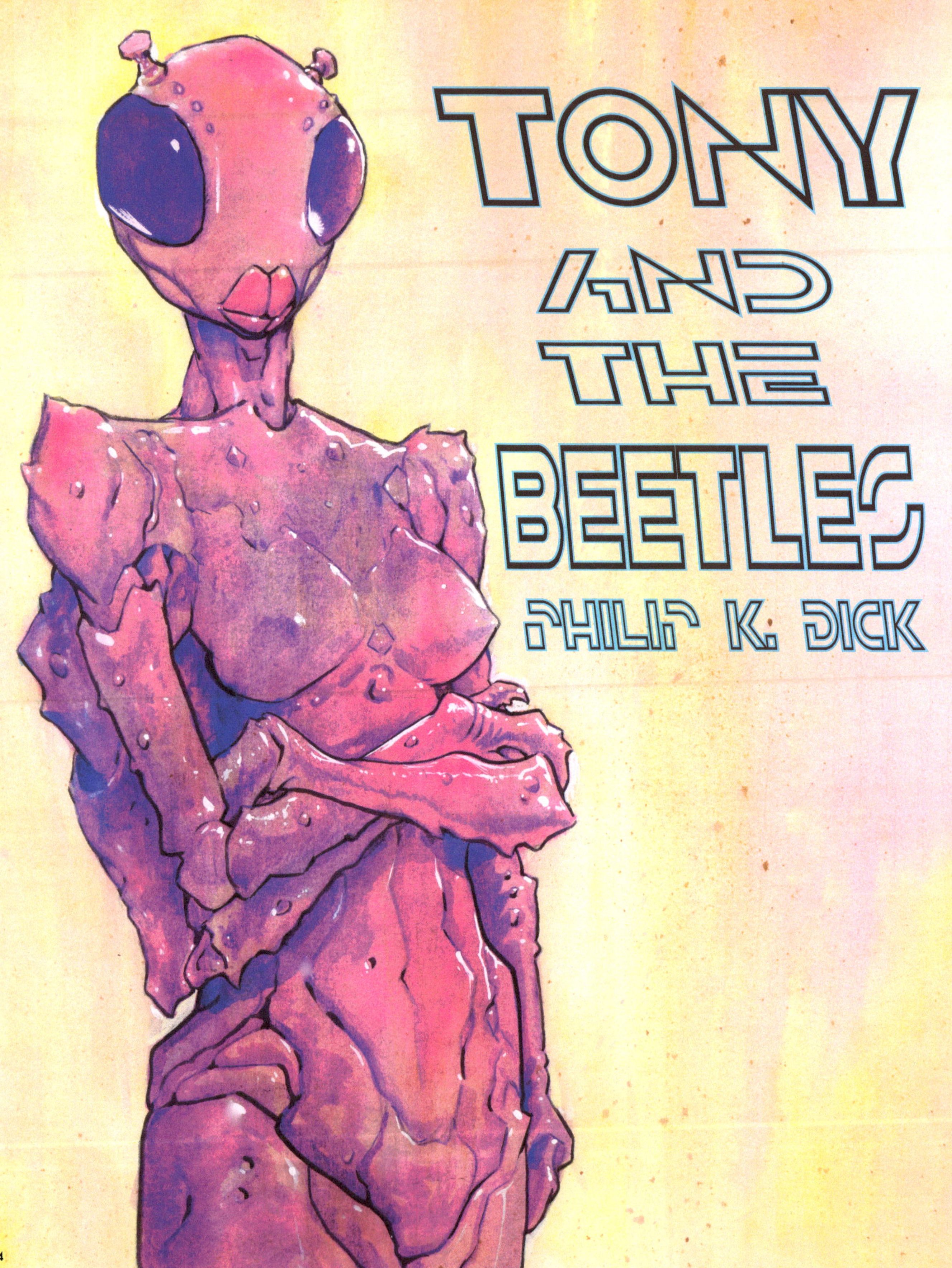
TONY
AND
THE
BEETLES
PHILIP K. DICK

REDDISH-YELLOW SUNLIGHT FILTERED THROUGH THE THICK QUARTZ WINDOWS INTO THE SLEEP-COMPARTMENT.

Tony Rossi yawned, stirred a little, then opened his black eyes and sat up quickly. With one motion he tossed the covers back and slid to the warm metal floor. He clicked off his alarm clock and hurried to the closet.

It looked like a nice day. The landscape outside was motionless, undisturbed by winds or dust-shift. The boy's heart pounded excitedly. He pulled his trousers on, zipped up the reinforced mesh, struggled into his heavy canvas shirt, and then sat down on the edge of the cot to tug on his boots. He closed the seams around their tops and then did the same with his gloves. Next he adjusted the pressure on his pump unit and strapped it between his shoulder blades. He grabbed his helmet from the dresser, and he was ready for the day.

In the dining-compartment his mother and father had finished breakfast. Their voices drifted to him as he clattered down the ramp. A disturbed murmur; he paused to listen. What were they talking about? Had he done something wrong, again?

And then he caught it. Behind their voices was another voice. Static and crackling pops. The all-system audio signal from Rigel IV. They had it turned up full blast; the dull thunder of the monitor's voice boomed loudly. The war. Always the war. He sighed, and stepped out into the dining-compartment.

"Morning," his father muttered.

"Good morning, dear," his mother said absently. She sat with her head turned to one side, wrinkles of concentration webbing her forehead. Her thin lips were drawn together in a tight line of concern. His father had pushed his dirty dishes back and was smoking, elbows on the table, dark hairy arms bare and muscular. He was scowling, intent on the jumbled roar from the speaker above the sink.

"How's it going?" Tony asked. He slid into his chair and reached automatically for the ersatz grapefruit. "Any news from Orion?"

Neither of them answered. They didn't hear him. He began to eat his grapefruit. Outside, beyond the little metal and plastic housing unit, sounds of activity grew. Shouts and muffled crashes, as rural merchants and their trucks rumbled along the highway toward Karnet. The reddish daylight swelled; Betelgeuse was rising quietly and majestically.

"Nice day," Tony said. "No flux wind. I think I'll go down to the n-quarter awhile. We're building a neat spaceport, a model, of course, but we've been able to get enough materials to lay out strips for—"

With a savage snarl his father reached out and struck the audio roar immediately died. "I knew it!" He got up and moved angrily away from the table. "I told them it would happen. They shouldn't have moved so soon. Should have built up Class A supply bases, first."

"Isn't our main fleet moving in from Bellatrix?" Tony's mother fluttered anxiously. "According to last night's summary the worst that can happen is Orion IX and X will be dumped."

Joseph Rossi laughed harshly. "The hell with last night's summary. They know as well as I do what's happening."

"What's happening?" Tony echoed, as he pushed aside his grapefruit and began to ladle out dry cereal. "Are we losing the battle?"

"Yes!" His father's lips twisted. "Earthmen, losing to—to beetles. I told them. But they couldn't wait. My God, there's ten good years left in this system. Why'd they have to push on? Everybody knew Orion would be tough. The whole damn beetle fleet's strung out around there. Waiting for us. And we have to barge right in."

"But nobody ever thought beetles would fight," Leah Rossi protested mildly. "Everybody thought they'd just fire a few blasts and then—"

"They have to fight! Orion's the last jump-off. If they don't fight here, where the hell can they fight?" Rossi swore savagely. "Of course they're fighting. We have all their planets except the inner Orion string—not that they're worth much, but it's the principle of the thing. If we'd built up strong supply bases, we could have broken up the beetle fleet and really clobbered it."

"Don't say 'beetle,'" Tony murmured, as he finished his cereal. "They're Pas-udeti, same as here. The word 'beetle' comes from Betelgeuse. An Arabian word we invented ourselves."

Joe Rossi's mouth opened and closed. "What are you, a goddamn beetle-lover?"

"Joe," Leah snapped. "For heaven's sake."

Rossi moved toward the door. "If I was ten years younger I'd be out there. I'd really show those shiny-shelled insects what the hell they're up against. Them and their junky beat-up old hulks. Converted freighters!" His eyes blazed. "When I think of them shooting down Terran cruisers with our boys in them—"

"Orion's their system," Tony murmured.

"Their system! When the hell did you get to be an authority on space law? Why, I ought to—" He broke off, choked with rage. "My own kid," he muttered. "One more crack out of you today and I'll hang one on you you'll feel the rest of the week."

Tony pushed his chair back. "I won't be around here today. I'm going into Karnet, with my EEP."

"Yeah, to play with beetles!"

Tony said nothing. He was already sliding his helmet in place and snapping the clamps tight. As he pushed through the back door, into the lock membrane, he unscrewed his oxygen tap and set the tank filter into action. An automatic response, conditioned by a lifetime spent on a colony planet in an alien system.

A faint flux wind caught at him and swept yellow-red dust around his boots. Sunlight glittered from the metal roof of his family's housing unit, one of endless rows of squat boxes set in the sandy slope, protected by the line of ore-refining installations against the horizon. He made an impatient signal, and from the storage shed his EEP came gliding out, catching the sunlight on its chrome trim.

"We're going down into Karnet," Tony said, unconsciously slipping into the Pas dialect. "Hurry up!"

The EEP took up its position behind him, and he started briskly down the slope, over the shifting sand, toward the road. There were quite a few traders out, today. It was a good day for the market; only a fourth of the year was fit for travel. Betelgeuse was an erratic and undependable sun, not at all like Sol (according to the edutapes, fed to Tony four hours a day, six days a week—he had never seen Sol himself).

He reached the noisy road. Pas-udeti were everywhere. Whole groups of them, with their primitive combustion-driven trucks, battered and filthy, motors grinding protestingly. He waved at the trucks as they pushed past him. After a moment one slowed down. It was piled with tis, bundled heaps of gray vegetables dried, and prepared for the table. A staple of the Pas-udeti diet. Behind the wheel lounged a dark-faced elderly Pas, one arm over the open window, a rolled leaf between his lips. He was like all other Pas-udeti; lank and hard-shelled, encased in a brittle sheath in which he lived and died.

"You want a ride?" the Pas murmured—required protocol when an Earthman on foot was encountered.

"Is there room for my EEP?"

The Pas made a careless motion with his claw. "It can run behind." Sardonic amusement touched his ugly old face. "If it gets to Karnet we'll sell it for scrap. We can use a few condensers and relay tubing. We're short on electronic maintenance stuff."

"I know," Tony said solemnly, as he climbed into the cabin of the truck. "It's all been sent to the big repair base at Orion I. For your warfleet."

Amusement vanished from the leathery face. "Yes, the warfleet." He turned away and started up the truck again. In the back, Tony's EEP had scrambled up on the load of tis and was gripping precariously with its magnetic lines.

Tony noticed the Pas-udeti's sudden change of expression, and he was puzzled. He started to speak to him—but now he noticed unusual quietness among the other Pas, in the other trucks, behind and in front of his own. The war, of course. It had swept through this system a century ago; these people had been left behind. Now all eyes were on Orion, on the battle between the Terran warfleet and the Pas-udeti collection of armed freighters.

"Is it true," Tony asked carefully, "that you're winning?"

The elderly Pas grunted. "We hear rumors."

Tony considered. "My father says Terra went ahead too fast. He says we should have consolidated. We didn't assemble adequate supply

bases. He used to be an officer, when he was younger. He was with the fleet for two years."

The Pas was silent a moment. "It's true," he said at last, "that when you're so far from home, supply is a great problem. We, on the other hand, don't have that. We have no distances to cover."

"Do you know anybody fighting?"

"I have distant relatives." The answer was vague; the Pas obviously didn't want to talk about it.

"Have you ever seen your warfleet?"

"Not as it exists now. When this system was defeated most of our units were wiped out. Remnants limped to Orion and joined the Orion fleet."

"Your relatives were with the remnants?"

"That's right."

"Then you were alive when this planet was taken?"

"Why do you ask?" The old Pas quivered violently. "What business is it of yours?"

Tony leaned out and watched the walls and buildings of Karnet grow ahead of them. Kar-net was an old city. It had stood thousands of years. The Pas-udeti civilization was stable; it had reached a certain point of technocratic development and then leveled off. The Pas had inter-system ships that had carried people and freight between planets in the days before the Terran Confederation. They had combustion-driven cars, audiophones, a power network of a magnetic type. Their plumbing was satisfactory and their medicine was highly advanced. They had art forms, emotional and exciting. They had a vague religion.

"Who do you think will win the battle?" Tony asked.

"I don't know." With a sudden jerk the old Pas brought the truck to a crashing halt. "This is as far as I go. Please get out and take your EEP with you."

Tony faltered in surprise. "But aren't you going—?"

"No farther!"

Tony pushed the door open. He was vaguely uneasy; there was a hard, fixed expression on the leathery face, and the old creature's voice had a sharp edge he had never heard before. "Thanks," he murmured. He hopped down into the red dust and signaled his EEP. It released its magnetic lines, and instantly the truck started up with a roar, passing on inside the city.

Tony watched it go, still dazed. The hot dust lapped at his ankles; he automatically moved his feet and slapped at his trousers. A truck honked, and his EEP quickly moved him from the road, up to the level pedestrian ramp. Pas-udeti in swarms moved by, endless lines of rural people hurrying into Karnet on their daily business. A massive public bus had stopped by the gate and was letting off passengers. Male and female Pas. And children. They laughed and shouted; the sounds of their voices blended with the low hum of the city.

"Going in?" a sharp Pas-udeti voice sounded close behind him. "Keep moving—you're blocking the ramp."

It was a young female, with a heavy armload clutched in her claws. Tony felt embarrassed; female Pas had a certain telepathic ability, part of their sexual make-up. It was effective on Earthmen at close range.

"Here," she said. "Give me a hand."

Tony nodded his head, and the EEP accepted the female's heavy armload. "I'm visiting the city," Tony said, as they moved with the crowd toward the gates. "I got a ride most of the way, but the driver let me off out here."

"You're from the settlement?"

"Yes."

She eyed him critically. "You've always lived here, haven't you?"

"I was born here. My family came here from Earth four years before I was born. My father was an officer in the fleet. He earned an Emigration Priority."

"So you've never seen your own planet. How old are you?"

"Ten years. Terran."

"You shouldn't have asked the driver so many questions."

They passed through the decontamination shield and into the city. An information square loomed ahead; Pas men and women were packed around it. Moving chutes and transport cars rumbled everywhere. Buildings and ramps and open-air machinery; the city was sealed in a protective dust-proof envelope. Tony unfastened his helmet and clipped it to his belt. The air was stale-smelling, artificial, but usable.

"Let me tell you something," the young female said carefully, as she strode along the foot-ramp beside Tony. "I wonder if this is a good day for you to come into Karnet. I know you've been coming here regularly to play with your friends. But perhaps today you ought to stay at home, in your settlement."

"Why?"

"Because today everybody is upset."

"I know," Tony said. "My mother and father were upset. They were listening to the news from our base in the Rigel system."

"I don't mean your family. Other people are listening, too. These people here. My race."

"They're upset, all right," Tony admitted. "But I come here all the time. There's nobody to play with at the settlement, and anyhow we're working on a project."

"A model spaceport."

"That's right." Tony was envious. "I sure wish I was a telepath. It must be fun."

The female Pas-udeti was silent. She was deep in thought. "What would happen," she asked, "if your family left here and returned to Earth?"

"That couldn't happen. There's no room for us on Earth. C-bombs destroyed most of Asia and North America back in the Twentieth Century."

"Suppose you had to go back?"

Tony did not understand. "But we can't. Habitable portions of Earth are overcrowded. Our main problem is finding places for Terrans to live, in other systems." He added, "And anyhow,

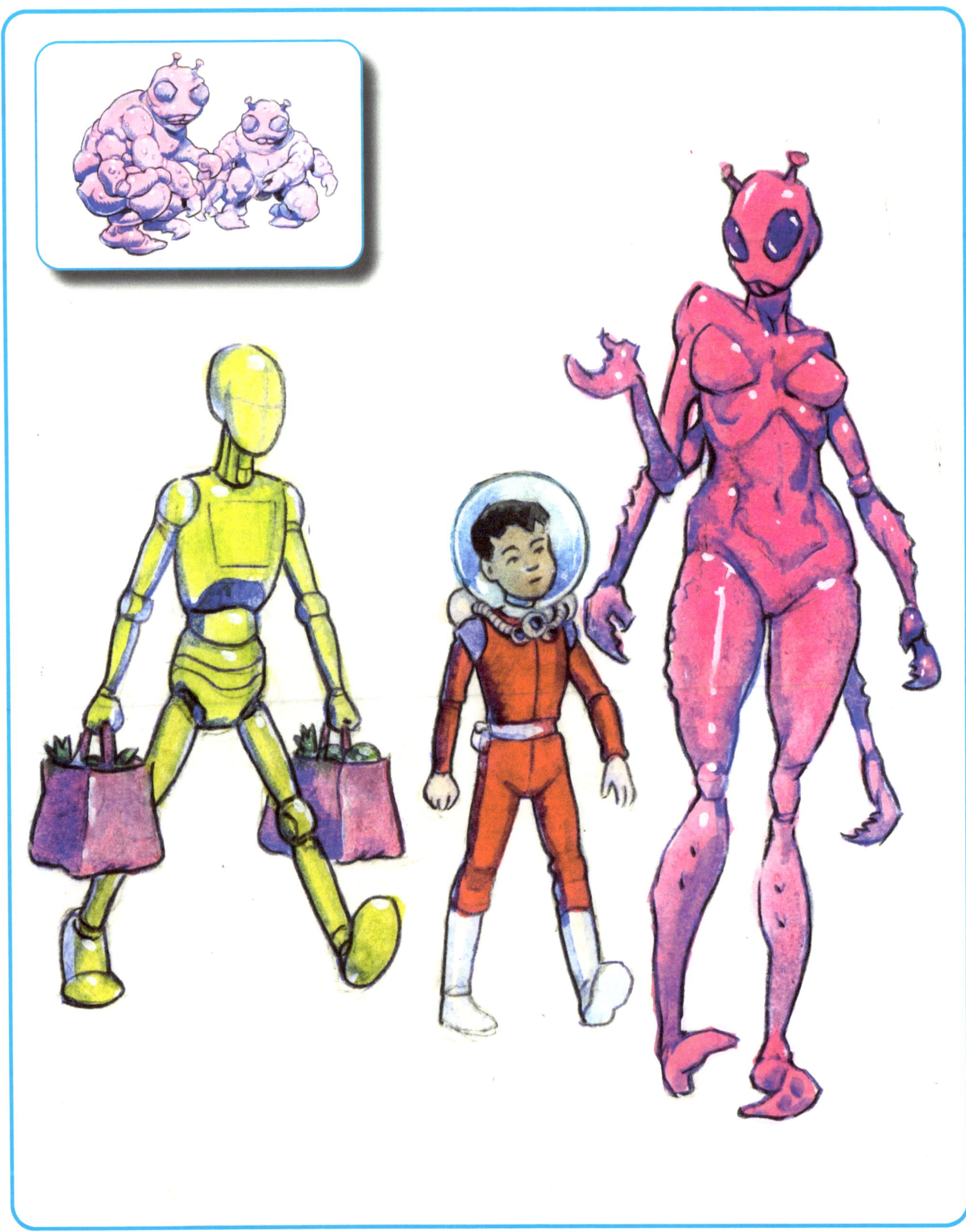

I don't particularly want to go to Terra. I'm used to it here. All my friends are here."

"I'll take my packages," the female said. "I go this other way, down this third-level ramp."

Tony nodded to his EEP and it lowered the bundles into the female's claws. She lingered a moment, trying to find the right words.

"Good luck," she said.

"With what?"

She smiled faintly, ironically. "With your model spaceport. I hope you and your friends get to finish it."

"Of course we'll finish it," Tony said, surprised. "It's almost done." What did she mean?

The Pas-udeti woman hurried off before he could ask her. Tony was troubled and uncertain; more doubts filled him. After a moment he headed slowly into the lane that took him toward the residential section of the city. Past the stores and factories, to the place where his friends lived.

The group of Pas-udeti children eyed him silently as he approached. They had been playing in the shade of an immense hengelo, whose ancient branches drooped and swayed with the air currents pumped through the city. Now they sat unmoving.

"I didn't expect you today," B'prith said, in an expressionless voice.

Tony halted awkwardly, and his EEP did the same. "How are things?" he murmured.

"Fine."

"I got a ride part way."

"Fine."

Tony squatted down in the shade. None of the Pas children stirred. They were small, not as large as Terran children. Their shells had not hardened, had not turned dark and opaque, like horn. It gave them a soft, unformed appearance, but at the same time it lightened their load. They moved more easily than their elders; they could hop and skip around, still. But they were not skipping right now.

"What's the matter?" Tony demanded. "What's wrong with everybody?"

No one answered.

"Where's the model?" he asked. "Have you fellows been working on it?"

After a moment Llyre nodded slightly.

Tony felt dull anger rise up inside him.

"Say something! What's the matter? What're you all mad about?"

"Mad?" B'prith echoed. "We're not mad."

Tony scratched aimlessly in the dust. He knew what it was. The war, again. The battle going on near Orion. His anger burst up wildly. "Forget the war. Everything was fine yesterday, before the battle."

"Sure," Llyre said. "It was fine."

Tony caught the edge to his voice. "It happened a hundred years ago. It's not my fault."

"Sure," B'prith said.

"This is my home. Isn't it? Haven't I got as much right here as anybody else? I was born here."

"Sure," Llyre said, tonelessly.

Tony appealed to them helplessly. "Do you have to act this way? You didn't act this way yesterday. I was here yesterday—all of us were here yesterday. What's happened since yesterday?"

"The battle," B'prith said.

"What difference does that make? Why does that change everything? There's always war. There've been battles all the time, as long as I can remember. What's different about this?"

B'prith broke apart a clump of dirt with his strong claws. After a moment he tossed it away and got slowly to his feet. "Well," he said thoughtfully, "according to our audio relay, it looks as if our fleet is going to win, this time."

"Yes," Tony agreed, not understanding. "My father says we didn't build up adequate supply bases. We'll probably have to fall back to...." And then the impact hit him. "You mean, for the first time in a hundred years—"

"Yes," Llyre said, also getting up. The others got up, too. They moved away from Tony, toward the near-by house. "We're winning. The Terran flank was turned, half an hour ago. Your right wing has folded completely."

Tony was stunned. "And it matters. It matters to all of you."

"Matters!" B'prith halted, suddenly blazing out in fury. "Sure it matters! For the first time—in a century. The first time in our lives we're beating you. We have you on the run, you—" He choked out the word, almost spat it out. "You white-grubs!"

They disappeared into the house. Tony sat gazing stupidly down at the ground, his hands still moving aimlessly. He had heard the word before, seen it scrawled on walls and in the dust near the settlement. White-grubs. The Pas term of derision for Terrans. Because of their soft-ness, their whiteness. Lack of hard shells. Pulpy, doughy skin. But they had never dared say it out loud, before. To an Earthman's face.

Beside him, his EEP stirred restlessly. Its intri-cate radio mechanism sensed the hostile atmo-sphere. Automatic relays were sliding into place; circuits were opening and closing.

"It's all right," Tony murmured, getting slowly up. "Maybe we'd better go back."

He moved unsteadily toward the ramp, com-pletely shaken. The EEP walked calmly ahead, its metal face blank and confident, feeling noth-ing, saying nothing. Tony's thoughts were a wild turmoil; he shook his head, but the crazy spin-ning kept up. He couldn't make his mind slow down, lock in place.

"Wait a minute," a voice said. B'prith's voice, from the open doorway. Cold and withdrawn, almost unfamiliar.

"What do you want?"

B'prith came toward him, claws behind his back in the formal Pas-udeti posture, used be-tween total strangers. "You shouldn't have come here, today."

"I know," Tony said.

B'prith got out a bit of tis stalk and began to roll it into a tube. He pretended to concentrate on it. "Look," he said. "You said you have a right here. But you don't."

"I—" Tony murmured.

"Do you understand why not? You said it isn't your fault. I guess not. But it's not my fault, ei-ther. Maybe it's nobody's fault. I've known you a long time."

"Five years. Terran."

B'prith twisted the stalk up and tossed it away. "Yesterday we played together. We worked on the spaceport. But we can't play today. My family said to tell you not to come here any more." He hesitated, and did not look Tony in the face. "I was going to tell you, anyhow. Before they said anything."

"Oh," Tony said.

"Everything that's happened today—the bat-tle, our fleet's stand. We didn't know. We didn't dare hope. You see? A century of running. First this system. Then the Rigel system, all the plan-ets. Then the other Orion stars. We fought here and there—scattered fights. Those that got away joined up. We supplied the base at Orion—you people didn't know. But there was no hope; at least, nobody thought there was." He was silent a moment. "Funny," he said, "what happens when your back's to the wall, and there isn't any further place to go. Then you have to fight."

"If our supply bases—" Tony began thickly, but B'prith cut him off savagely.

"Your supply bases! Don't you understand? We're beating you! Now you'll have to get out! All you white-grubs. Out of our system!"

Tony's EEP moved forward ominously. B'prith saw it. He bent down, snatched up a rock, and hurled it straight at the EEP. The rock clanged off the metal hull and bounced harmlessly away. B'prith snatched up another rock. Llyre and the others came quickly out of the house. An adult Pas loomed up behind them. Everything was happening too fast. More rocks crashed against the EEP. One struck Tony on the arm.

"Get out!" B'prith screamed. "Don't come back! This is our planet!" His claws snatched at Tony. "We'll tear you to pieces if you—"

Tony smashed him in the chest. The soft shell gave like rubber, and the Pas stumbled back. He wobbled and fell over, gasping and screeching.

"Beetle," Tony breathed hoarsely. Suddenly he was terrified. A crowd of Pas-udeti was forming rapidly. They surged on all sides, hostile faces, dark and angry, a rising thunder of rage.

More stones showered. Some struck the EEP, others fell around Tony, near his boots. One whizzed past his face. Quickly he slid his helmet in place. He was scared. He knew his EEP's E-signal had already gone out, but it would be minutes before a ship could come. Besides, there were other Earthmen in the city to be taken care of; there were Earthmen all over the planet. In all the cities. On all the twenty-three Betelgeuse planets. On the fourteen Rigel planets. On the other Orion planets.

"We have to get out of here," he muttered to the EEP. "Do something!"

A stone hit him on the helmet. The plastic cracked; air leaked out, and then the autoseal filmed over. More stones were falling. The Pas

swarmed close, a yelling, seething mass of black-sheathed creatures. He could smell them, the acrid body-odor of insects, hear their claws snap, feel their weight.

The EEP threw its heat beam on. The beam shifted in a wide band toward the crowd of Pasudeti. Crude hand weapons appeared. A clatter of bullets burst around Tony; they were firing at the EEP. He was dimly aware of the metal body beside him. A shuddering crash—the EEP was toppled over.

The crowd poured over it; the metal hull was lost from sight.

Like a demented animal, the crowd tore at the struggling EEP. A few of them smashed in its head; others tore off struts and shiny arm-sections. The EEP ceased struggling. The crowd moved away, panting and clutching jagged remains. They saw Tony.

As the first line of them reached for him, the protective envelope high above them shattered. A Terran scout ship thundered down, heat beam screaming. The crowd scattered in confusion, some firing, some throwing stones, others leaping for safety.

Tony picked himself up and made his way unsteadily toward the spot where the scout was landing.

"I'm sorry," Joe Rossi said gently. He touched his son on the shoulder. "I shouldn't have let you go down there today. I should have known."

Tony sat hunched over in the big plastic easy-chair. He rocked back and forth, face pale with shock. The scout ship which had rescued him had immediately headed back toward Karnet; there were other Earthmen to bring out, besides this first load. The boy said nothing. His mind was blank. He still heard the roar of the crowd, felt its hate—a century of pent-up fury and resentment. The memory drove out everything else; it was all around him, even now. And the sight of the floundering EEP, the metallic ripping sound, as its arms and legs were torn off and carried away.

His mother dabbed at his cuts and scratches with antiseptic. Joe Rossi shakily lit a cigarette and said, "If your EEP hadn't been along they'd have killed you. Beetles." He shuddered. "I never should have let you go down there. All this time.... They might have done it any time, any day. Knifed you. Cut you open with their filthy goddamn claws."

Below the settlement the reddish-yellow sunlight glinted on gunbarrels. Already, dull booms echoed against the crumbling hills. The defense ring was going into action. Black shapes darted and scurried up the side of the slope. Black patches moved out from Karnet, toward the Terran settlement, across the dividing line the Confederation surveyors had set up a century ago. Karnet was a bubbling pot of activity. The whole city rumbled with feverish excitement.

Tony raised his head. "They—they turned our flank."

"Yeah." Joe Rossi stubbed out his cigarette. "They sure did. That was at one o'clock. At two they drove a wedge right through the center of our line. Split the fleet in half. Broke it up—sent it running. Picked us off one by one as we fell back. Christ, they're like maniacs. Now that they've got the scent, the taste of our blood."

"But it's getting better," Leah fluttered. "Our main fleet units are beginning to appear."

"We'll get them," Joe muttered. "It'll take a while. But by God we'll wipe them out. Every last one of them. If it takes a thousand years. We'll follow every last ship down—we'll get them all." His voice rose in frenzy. "Beetles! Goddamn insects! When I think of them, trying to hurt my kid, with their filthy black claws—"

"If you were younger, you'd be in the line," Leah said. "It's not your fault you're too old. The heart strain's too great. You did your job. They can't let an older person take chances. It's not your fault."

Joe clenched his fists. "I feel so—futile. If there was only something I could do."

"The fleet will take care of them," Leah said soothingly. "You said so yourself. They'll hunt every one of them down. Destroy them all. There's nothing to worry about."

Joe sagged miserably. "It's no use. Let's cut it out. Let's stop kidding ourselves."

"What do you mean?"

"Face it! We're not going to win, not this time. We went too far. Our time's come."

There was silence.

Tony sat up a little. "When did you know?"

"I've known a long time."

"I found out today. I didn't understand, at first. This is—stolen ground. I was born here, but it's stolen ground."

"Yes. It's stolen. It doesn't belong to us."

"We're here because we're stronger. But now we're not stronger. We're being beaten."

"They know Terrans can be licked. Like anybody else." Joe Rossi's face was gray and flabby. "We took their planets away from them. Now they're taking them back. It'll be a while, of course. We'll retreat slowly. It'll be another five centuries going back. There're a lot of systems between here and Sol."

Tony shook his head, still uncomprehending. "Even Llyre and B'prith. All of them. Waiting for their time to come. For us to lose and go away again. Where we came from."

Joe Rossi paced back and forth. "Yeah, we'll be retreating from now on. Giving ground, instead of taking it. It'll be like this today—losing fights, draws. Stalemates and worse."

He raised his feverish eyes toward the ceiling of the little metal housing unit, face wild with passion and misery.

"But, by God, we'll give them a run for their money. All the way back! Every inch!"

PHILIP KINDRED DICK explored the nature of reality, perception, and altered states of consciousness. His seminal works include 44 novels and approximately 121 short stories, influencing cyberpunk, science fiction, and movies for the past seventy years.

CULLEN BUNN is best known for his work on comic books such as **Uncanny X-Men, X-Men: Blue, Magneto** and various **Deadpool** miniseries for Marvel Comics, and his creator-owned series **The Damned** and **The Sixth Gun** for Oni Press and **Harrow County** for Dark Horse Comics, as well as his middle reader horror novel Crooked Hills, and his short story work collection **Creeping Stones & Other Stories**.

JOHN SHIRLEY is the author of numerous novels, including **Demons, Wetbones, Cellars, City Come A-Walkin', A Splendid Chaos, Bioshock: Rapture, Demons, The Other End** and the Eclipse cyberpunk trilogy, **A Song Called Youth**, (Dover Books). His newest novels are **Stormland** and **A Sorcerer of Atlantis**. His story collection **Black Butterflies** won the Bram Stoker Award. His new story collection is **The Feverish**

Stars. He is co-screenwriter of **The Crow** and has written teleplays and animation. Jackanapes Press released his book of weird poetry, **The Voice of the Burning House** and will soon be releasing the new expanded edition of his story collection, **Really Really Really Really Weird Stories**. He wrote the lyrics for five songs on the Blue Oyster Cult's new hit album, **The Symbol Remains**.

NICK MAMATAS is the author of several novels, including **Move Under Ground, I Am Providence,** and **The Second Shooter.** His short fiction has appeared in Best American Mystery Stories, Year's Best Science Fiction and Fantasy, Tor.com, and many other venues. Much of it was recently collected in **The People's Republic of Everything.** Nick is also an anthologist; he co-edited the Bram Stoker Award-winner **Haunted Legends** with Ellen Datlow, and the Locus Award nominees **The Future is Japanese** and **Hanzai Japan** with Masumi Washington. He recently collected Lovecraftian fictions in the sublime mode in the anthology **Wonder and Glory Forever**. Nick's fiction and editorial work has been variously nominated for the Stoker, Hugo, World Fantasy, and Shirley Jackson awards.

JOHN WAYNE COMUNALE Lives in Houston Texas to prepare himself for the heat in Hell. He is the author of **Death Pacts and Left-Hand Paths, Scummer, As Seen On T.V., Sinkhole, The Cycle** and more. He hosts the weekly storytelling podcast John Wayne Lied to You, co-hosts the podcast Vital Social Issues 'N Stuff with Kris and John Wayne with horror author Kristopher Triana, and fronts the punk rock disaster **johnwayneisdead**. He currently travels around the country giving truly unique and most excellent performances of the written word.

ERICA L. SATIFKA has short fiction in **Clarkesworld, Interzone, Nature,** and many other places. Her 2021 debut collection **How to Get to Apocalypse and Other Disasters** was named one of the best SF books of the year by the Washington Post and Tor.com, and she is the recipient of the 2017 British Fantasy Award for Best Newcomer. She lives in Portland, Oregon.

MIKE DUBISCH has designed characters and illustrated windows into multiple universes, from **Star Wars** to **Dungeons and Dragons, Aliens VS Predator, The Wheel Of Time,** and the **Cthulhu Mythos.** In **Forbidden Futures** magazine, Mike collaborates with the world's greatest genre fiction writers to help create new universes every issue. A veteran of role playing games, underground horror comix, pulp science fiction magazines and role playing game miniatures, Mike has been a professional illustrator for over three decades, and is known as a visionary fantasy illustrator, surrealist and graphic novelist.

CODY GOODFELLOW has written eight novels, and co-wrote three more with New York Times bestselling author John Skipp. His first two collections, **Silent Weapons For Quiet Wars and All-Monster Action,** each received the Wonderland Book Award. He wrote, co-produced and scored the short Lovecraftian hygiene films **Stay At Home Dad** and **Baby Got Bass**, which may be viewed on YouTube. As an actor, he has appeared in numerous short films, TV shows, music videos and commercials. He is also a cofounder of Perilous Press, an occasional micropublisher of modern cosmic horror. He lives in San Diego, California.

ODDNESS (author, publisher, producer) originates from unknown lands, and dabbles in modular synths and playing video games.